Fletcher and Zenobia

NEW YORK REVIEW BOOKS
ILLUSTRATED BY EDWARD GOREY

VICTORIA CHESS AND EDWARD GOREY

Fletcher and Zenobia

ILLUSTRATED BY VICTORIA CHESS

The New York Review Children's Collection
New York

THIS IS A NEW YORK REVIEW BOOK
PUBLISHED BY THE NEW YORK REVIEW OF BOOKS
435 Hudson Street, New York, NY 10014
www.nyrb.com

A catalog record for this book is available from the Library of Congress

ISBN 978-1-59017-963-5

Manufactured in China
1 3 5 7 9 10 8 6 4 2

To George

Once there was a cat named Fletcher who lived in the largest and tallest tree for miles around. He had run up it in a moment of thoughtless abandon, and ever since had been unable to get down again.

The tree also harbored a vast, brass-bound leather trunk. Fletcher often wondered how *it* had got there.

It contained all sorts of things, including a collection of hats for all occasions. Alas, not one single one had arisen as long as Fletcher had been in the tree.

In fact, there was almost nothing to do but walk back and forth along the branches or watch the clouds going past in the sky.

One day, however, Fletcher was rummaging about in the depths of the trunk when he came across a papier-mâché egg larger than himself. It was covered with orange roses on a violet ground, and was rather dusty; a band of tarnished gold-filigree paper went round its middle.

"Ho!" said Fletcher. "I never saw *that* before."

With some difficulty he heaved the egg from the trunk and wedged it in the fork of a branch. As he was attacking it with a duster, he noticed a label pasted to it near the top. The writing was much faded, but he decided that it read: *For the attic (unwanted by Mabel)*.

"Is there someone there?" said a faint voice from inside the egg.

"Is there someone *there?*" said Fletcher, who was startled.

"Only Echo," said the voice, sadly.

"No, my name is Fletcher."

"Mine is Zenobia," said the voice. "How do you do?"

"How do you do?" said Fletcher.

"Not too well," said Zenobia. "My feet are asleep. Do you think you might open the egg and let me out?"

"Of course. I'll go and get an axe."

There was a muffled shriek. "That won't be necessary. It comes apart in the middle. Under the gold paper. Twist!"

After twisting in the wrong direction until he was quite short of breath, Fletcher realized his mistake and at last succeeded in removing the top.

Tottering slightly (for her feet were all pins and needles) but elegant withal, an old-fashioned doll stepped from the bottom half of the egg. She was dressed in mauve velvet, and though her face was plain, the ribbons on her gown and the flowers on her hat were stylish indeed—not to mention her buttons.

"How do you do again," they both said together and ceremoniously shook hands.

"What were you doing inside that egg?" asked Fletcher.

"Mine is a long, sad story," said Zenobia, wriggling first one foot and then the other to restore the circulation. "Fortunately, I can remember almost none of it."

"Who was Mabel?"

"An unfeeling child. You will not be surprised to learn she had fat wrists." Zenobia shuddered. "But let us not speak of her."

She looked around her with puzzled interest.

"We are in a tree," said Fletcher.

"A perfect place for a sunny summer afternoon," said Zenobia. "Where do you live otherwise?"

Fletcher explained there wasn't any otherwise.

"I don't think I should much care for it here on a rainy night in winter. Besides, the great world is out there below."

Fletcher sighed; he had nearly forgotten it entirely.

"We shall have to find a way to get down," said Zenobia. She opened her parasol and peered at the result. "No, that won't do."

She sat down and dangled her legs disconsolately. "Oh, dearie me."

"We could have a party," said Fletcher to cheer her up, uttering the first thing that came into his head.

"Why not?" said Zenobia, uttering the first thing that came into hers.

So they set to, and by the time the sun had gone down, Zenobia had baked a lemon cake with five layers, which she covered with raspberry icing and walnuts and decorated with green and blue candles ("Perhaps it's one of our birthdays," she said), and Fletcher had made four quarts of peach ice cream in the freezer and three gallons of pineapple and strawberry punch in the silver punch bowl.

By the time the moon had risen, they had blown up what seemed like at least several hundred balloons, although really there were only twenty-seven.

As they were getting their breaths back, Fletcher thought of the hats. "This *is* an occasion, isn't it?" he asked.

"Indeed it is," said Zenobia.

Fletcher went and got the hats from the trunk. "Which ones ought we to wear?"

Zenobia surveyed the hats, and frowned. "I'm afraid I'm not quite certain."

"Then let's wear the ones we like best."

So after much trying-on and taking-off of hats, exchanging of opinions, and changing of minds, Zenobia at last chose one for being in a gondola on the Grand Canal of Venice, and Fletcher picked one to wear while being presented to a maharajah in the course of an elephant hunt.

A little while later the party was in full swing and Zenobia was teaching Fletcher how to reverse while waltzing.

"Now bring your left foot," said Zenobia, "around in back of—"

"What was that?" said Fletcher.

"No, your *left* foot. What was what?"

"Are you sure you mean my left foot? That *flumpety flumpety* noise."

"I don't hear anything. Yes. But not in front; in back—"

"It's getting louder. I'm going to end up facing in the wrong—"

"I believe I *do* hear something. It's going *flumpety flumpety*…"

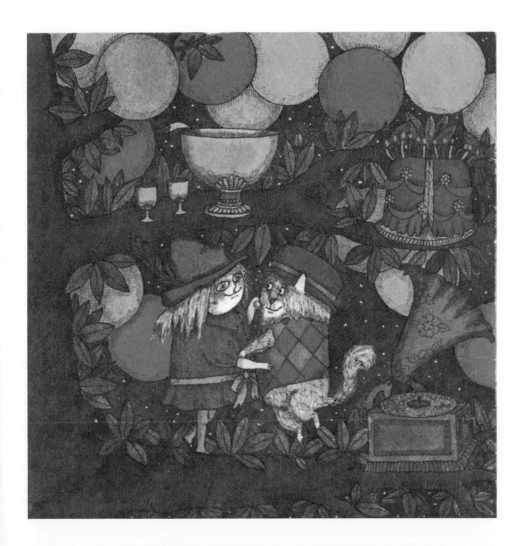

Just then a branch above their heads trembled slightly as something landed on it and a moment later a large, brightly colored moth appeared among the leaves and looked down at them.

"Oh, we have a guest," said Zenobia. "How delightful!"

"It's a party," said Fletcher, "with dancing and refreshments. Would you like to come to it?"

"How kind of you to invite me!" said the moth and flew down in a graceful semicircle to join them.

In a twinkling he drained the cup of punch Fletcher handed him and asked Zenobia to dance. Fletcher rewound the gramophone and off they went. Zenobia was surprised to find how tall the moth was when he stood up. When the record came to an end, Fletcher refilled everybody's cup.

Fletcher and Zenobia waltzed again; after several more false attempts, Fletcher at last succeeded in mastering the reverse. The moth, meanwhile, had a large dish of ice cream, and after that, a second, even larger.

Fletcher put a new needle in the gramophone and Zenobia and the moth danced a second time. Whether it was the dazzling combination of candlelight and moonlight or what, to Zenobia he really seemed taller than he had a few minutes ago.

Fletcher and Zenobia waltzed a third time: Fletcher's reverses were now absolutely brilliant and they both got quite giddy from doing them so often. The moth applauded each time in between bites of an enormous piece of cake.

Once more Zenobia and the moth danced to-gether. Although it was getting late and she had been dancing since the party began, she felt sure the moth was now taller than ever. Fletcher began to yawn behind the gramophone horn.

While the moth, at their insistence, was finishing what was left of the refreshments, Fletcher and Zenobia one by one untied the balloons and watched them float away on the gentle breeze.

"Wouldn't it be lovely," said Zenobia drowsily, "if we could just float away from the tree that way too?"

"How true!" said Fletcher, whose eyes were closing.

As they fell asleep, they could hear the moth crunching away on the last of the walnuts.

In the morning when Zenobia woke up, she gave a small scream. She was looking at a bewildering arrangement of large colored spots. What could they be? "Fletcher! Fletcher!" she cried. "Something has happened, but I don't know what."

A familiar face suddenly appeared at the edge of the spots. "It's his wings," said Fletcher in a whisper. "He's grown in the night. He's now perfectly enormous."

"I *thought* that was what was happening all along," said Zenobia, "but it seemed so unlikely. Of course, the cake was frightfully rich. All those eggs! All that butter and sugar!"

"And all that cream!" said Fletcher. "What beautiful spots!"

At that the moth woke up and stretched his feelers. "Good morning!"

"Good morning," said Fletcher and Zenobia.

"What a lovely party that was! Thank you so much for having me. I don't know when I've eaten quite so much."

"We're glad you liked it," said Zenobia.

"You've grown," said Fletcher.

The moth looked up at his wings. "So I have. It will be days of just nibbling before I get back to my proper size. Ah well, that's what parties are!"

The moth looked about him. "Do you live in this tree? It's a delightful place for a party, but what do you do when there isn't one?"

Fletcher explained their predicament.

"Oh, but I could easily carry you away on my back," said the moth. "That is, if you would care to come."

"It's our fondest wish," said Fletcher and Zenobia joyfully.

"Shall we be off, then?" said the moth.

They waited only long enough to gather up all the hats and to put on goggles to protect them against the wind (there was a third pair for the moth, who was terribly pleased), before settling themselves on the moth's back. He fanned his great wings several times and then they were no longer in the tree.

And so Fletcher and Zenobia flew away to the great world—and who knew what splendid occasions?

VICTORIA CHESS was born in Chicago in 1939 and attended the Kokoschka School of Art in Salzburg, Austria, and the Boston Museum School. The illustrator of more than a hundred books for children, Chess was awarded the Brooklyn Art Books for Children citation from the Brooklyn Museum and the Brooklyn Public Library in 1973 for *Fletcher and Zenobia*, and the 1975 American Institute of Graphic Arts Book Show Award for her illustrations for *Bugs*, a book of poems by Mary Ann Hoberman. She lives in Cambridge, Massachusetts, and the south of France.

EDWARD GOREY (1925–2000) was born in Chicago. He studied briefly at the Art Institute of Chicago, spent three years in the army, and attended Harvard College, where he majored in French literature. In 1953 Gorey published *The Unstrung Harp*, the first of his many books, which include *The Curious Sofa*, *The Haunted Tea-Cosy*, and *The Epiplectic Bicycle*. In addition to illustrating his own stories, Gorey provided drawings to many books for both children and adults. Of these, New York Review Books has published *The Haunted Looking Glass*, a collection of Gorey's favorite ghost stories; *The War of the Worlds* by H. G. Wells; *Men and Gods* by Rex Warner; and *Three Ladies Beside the Sea* and *He Was There from the Day We Moved In* by Rhoda Levine.

TITLES IN THE
NEW YORK REVIEW CHILDREN'S COLLECTION

ESTHER AVERILL
Captains of the City Streets
The Hotel Cat
Jenny and the Cat Club
Jenny Goes to Sea
Jenny's Birthday Book
Jenny's Moonlight Adventure
The School for Cats

JAMES CLOYD BOWMAN
Pecos Bill: The Greatest Cowboy of All Time

PALMER BROWN
Beyond the Pawpaw Trees
Cheerful
Hickory
The Silver Nutmeg
Something for Christmas

SHEILA BURNFORD
Bel Ria: Dog of War

MARY CHASE
Loretta Mason Potts

CARLO COLLODI and FULVIO TESTA
Pinocchio

INGRI and EDGAR PARIN D'AULAIRE
D'Aulaires' Book of Animals
D'Aulaires' Book of Norse Myths
D'Aulaires' Book of Trolls
Foxie: The Singing Dog
The Terrible Troll-Bird
Too Big
The Two Cars

EILÍS DILLON
The Island of Horses
The Lost Island

ELEANOR FARJEON
The Little Bookroom

PENELOPE FARMER
Charlotte Sometimes

PAUL GALLICO
The Abandoned

LEON GARFIELD
The Complete Bostock and Harris
Leon Garfield's Shakespeare Stories
Smith: The Story of a Pickpocket

RUMER GODDEN
An Episode of Sparrows
The Mousewife

MARIA GRIPE and HARALD GRIPE
The Glassblower's Children

LUCRETIA P. HALE
The Peterkin Papers

RUSSELL and LILLIAN HOBAN
The Sorely Trying Day

RUTH KRAUSS and MARC SIMONT
The Backward Day

DOROTHY KUNHARDT
Junket Is Nice
Now Open the Box

MUNRO LEAF and ROBERT LAWSON
Wee Gillis

RHODA LEVINE and EVERETT AISON
Arthur

RHODA LEVINE and EDWARD GOREY
He Was There from the Day We Moved In
Three Ladies Beside the Sea

BETTY JEAN LIFTON
and EIKOH HOSOE
Taka-chan and I

ASTRID LINDGREN
Mio, My Son
Seacrow Island

NORMAN LINDSAY
The Magic Pudding

ERIC LINKLATER
The Wind on the Moon

J. P. MARTIN
Uncle
Uncle Cleans Up

JOHN MASEFIELD
The Box of Delights
The Midnight Folk

WILLIAM MCCLEER
and WARREN CHAPPELL
Wolf Story

JEAN MERRILL and RONNI SOLBERT
The Elephant Who Liked to Smash Small Cars
The Pushcart War

E. NESBIT
The House of Arden

ALFRED OLLIVANT's
Bob, Son of Battle: The Last Gray Dog of Kenmuir
A New Version by LYDIA DAVIS